Pat's Promise

By Sandy Asher

Illustrated by Susan Tang

A
LITTLE APPLE
PAPERBACK

SCHOLASTIC INC.

New York Toronto London Auckland Sydney

For Jean Williams

ISBN 0-590-41844-0

Text copyright © 1990 by Sandy Asher.

Illustrations copyright © 1990 by Scholastic Inc.

All rights reserved. Published by Scholastic Inc.

APPLE PAPERBACKS is a registered trademark of Scholastic Inc.

12 11 10 9 8 7 6 5 4 3 2   0 1 2 3 4/9

Printed in the U.S.A.

First Scholastic printing, January 1990

Contents

Also look for

Ballet One #1   Best Friends Get Better

Chapter One
The First Promise

"So you're really going to be a horse?" asked Mrs. Parker. She was in Pat's room, helping her get ready for Ballet One.

"A *ballet circus* horse, Mom," said Pat.

"I don't know," said Mrs. Parker, shaking her head. "Ballet One isn't what I thought it would be."

"What did you think it would be?" asked Pat.

"Pretty girls in pretty costumes," said Mrs. Parker.

"Better not tell Paul and Stanley that," said Pat. "They're in Ballet One."

Mrs. Parker pulled a brush through Pat's light yellow hair. It hit a tangle.

"Ouch!" Pat yelped.

"Hold still," Mrs. Parker said, "I'm almost finished."

She divided Pat's hair into two bunches. She put a rubber band around each one. Then she tied them up with a pair of pink ribbons. "There!" she said.

Pat made a dash for the dance bag in her closet. "Hurry," she said. "I don't want to be late like last Saturday."

Then the phone rang.

"Just when we're in a rush," said Mrs. Parker. "And I don't know where I put my car keys."

"I'll get it," said Pat. She dropped her dance bag and ran to answer the phone.

"Pattycake?" said the voice at the other end.

"Daddy!" said Pat. "Hi!"

"Hi, sweetheart," said Mr. Parker. "How's tricks?"

"Tricks are fine," said Pat. "How's tricks with you?"

"Not so good," said Mr. Parker. "I'm

afraid I have bad news. It's about Visiting Day at Ballet One next Saturday. I may not be able to come."

"But you promised," said Pat.

"I know, Pattycake," said Mr. Parker. "And I'm sorry. Something's come up at work. I have to go to Omaha for some important meetings. I won't get back until Saturday night."

"But you promised," Pat said again. It was all she could think of to say.

"If there's any way I can keep that promise, I will, Pat," her father said. "But we'd better not count on it."

"When will you know for sure?" asked Pat.

"Monday," said Mr. Parker. "I'll call you then, okay?"

"Okay," Pat said softly. "Try to come, Daddy. Try *hard*."

Mrs. Parker came down the hall, patting the pockets of her skirt. "Who was it?" she asked just as Pat hung up the phone.

"Daddy," said Pat. "He may not come to

Visiting Day next week. He may have to go to Omaha instead."

"Oh, that's too bad," said Mrs. Parker. "I'm sorry."

Pat sighed. Everybody was sorry. But that didn't help one bit.

Mrs. Parker opened the door of the hall closet. She began fishing in all the coat pockets. "Now, where did I put those keys?" she muttered.

Pat sighed again. In their old house across town, her father kept all the keys on a board in the kitchen. Then he and her mother got divorced. He moved away first and took the board with him. Then Pat and her mom moved. They needed a new board for their new house.

"Here they are!" said Mrs. Parker. "Let's go. We're really late now!"

Pat grabbed her dance bag again and raced out to the garage ahead of her mother. Mrs. Parker backed the car out of the driveway.

"Ellie's parents will be at Visiting Day,"

Pat said. "Both of them. Mary's whole family will be there. Two parents and four brothers."

Mrs. Parker made a right turn at the corner and headed toward Campbell Street. Miss Drew's School of Dance was all the way down Campbell, at the South Oaks Shopping Center.

"Pat," she said, "you know your father would like to be there, too. But he has to work."

Pat turned away. She didn't want to talk about that. She looked out the window. The trees were just beginning to turn yellow and orange and red. Springfield looked pretty.

"Mary and Ellie and I are best friends," she said, changing the subject.

"I thought you told me David Sims was Ellie's best friend," Mrs. Parker said.

"He is at school," said Pat. "But not at Ballet One. Ellie and Mary and I are the only ones in third grade at Rountree School *and* in Ballet One. We do everything to-gether."

"Nobody can do *everything* together," said Mrs. Parker. "Not even if they want to."

Pat thought about her father. But it made her feel bad again. Mrs. Parker stopped at a red light. I'll count to ten, Pat thought. If the light turns green before ten, Daddy will be able to come to Visiting Day. She counted to herself as slowly as she could. But the light stayed red until she'd counted to ten three times.

Chapter Two
A Talk with Miss Drew

"Where have you been?" Ellie Bell shouted as Pat hurried inside Miss Drew's School of Dance. Ellie and Mary Stone raced across the room to meet Pat.

"We thought you'd never get here," said Mary.

"My mom couldn't find her keys again," said Pat. She didn't want to tell them about her father's phone call.

"One more week until Visiting Day," Ellie said.

"Every time I think about it, I get butterflies in my stomach," said Mary. "Everyone will be here, watching us. And I'm not sure of our dance."

"I hope David Sims doesn't make me laugh," said Ellie. "You know what? He says his parents want to come, too!"

"I hope my brothers don't laugh *at* us," said Mary.

Four brothers, thought Pat as she put on her ballet slippers.

Pat's throat felt lumpy. She swallowed hard. Everyone had lots of people coming on Visiting Day. Everyone but her.

"Time to begin, girls and boys," said Miss Drew. The class hurried to line up at the *barre*.

Miss Drew was wearing all pink today: leotard, tights, ballet skirt, and slippers. They looked nice against her brown skin.

"First position. *Plié*," said Miss Drew.

Mr. Ross played the piano. Miss Drew showed the class how to put their heels together. Slowly they bent their knees.

Every week, Ballet One got a little harder. There were more and more steps to remember. Their names were all in French. *Plié* meant to bend your knees.

"Straight backs," Miss Drew reminded the class. "Tummies tucked in. Chins up."

If I do every step perfectly today, Pat told herself, Daddy will be able to come next week. But it was hard to remember everything at once.

"Second position," said Miss Drew. "Brush your foot along the floor, Nancy. Ellie, point your toes. Lift your arm, Paul. Not that high! That's it. And *plié.*"

Pat always tried to do the steps exactly like Miss Drew. Today she would be perfect. She just had to be.

"Stop looking at your feet, Pat," Miss Drew said. "Don't worry. They won't fall off."

Miss Drew smiled. The class laughed. Pat knew Miss Drew was just making a joke. But she burst into tears anyway. She couldn't help it.

Mr. Ross stopped playing the piano. The whole class turned around to look at Pat. The tears kept coming. Pat faced the *barre* so no one could see her. But in that big, bright room filled with mirrors, there was no place to hide.

Miss Drew put her arm around Pat's shoulders. "Go on with the exercise," she told the others. "Mary, please lead the class."

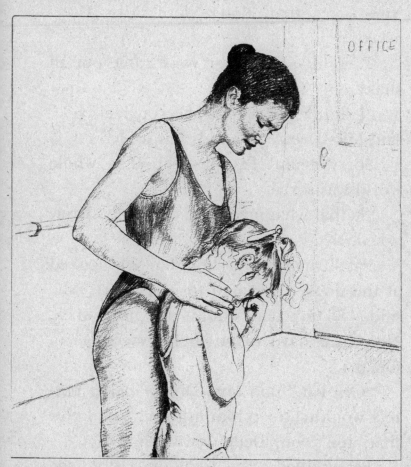

Mr. Ross played the music for *pliés* again. Miss Drew took Pat into her office. It was a tiny room behind the piano. The two of them sat down on a fat, blue sofa.

"I want to help you dance better, Pat. You know that, don't you?" Miss Drew asked.

"Yes," Pat said. Her voice came out all shaky.

"I didn't mean to make you feel bad," said Miss Drew. "If I did, I'm sorry."

Sorry again! Pat thought. The whole world was sorry.

"Is that what made you cry?" Miss Drew asked.

Pat shrugged her shoulders and looked at the floor. "I wanted to be perfect," she said. "So my dad would visit next week. Now he'll have to go to his meetings in Omaha."

"Oh, Pat," said Miss Drew. "Being perfect wouldn't keep him in town. You know that, don't you? Deep down inside?"

Pat nodded. "But what *can* I do?" she

asked. "He might not have to go. I want to do something to make sure."

"You can't make other people do things your way," said Miss Drew. "Sometimes all you can do is try to change your own feelings so that you don't feel so bad."

"But I *do* feel bad," Pat said. She poked her finger at a piece of white fuzz on the blue sofa.

"Then maybe dancing can change how you feel," said Miss Drew. "Do you know what always cheers me up? Dreadful day dances."

Pat smiled. "How can there be dreadful day dances?" she asked.

"You'll see," said Miss Drew. "Come on. I'll show you. As soon as we finish warming up."

Chapter Three
Dreadful Day Dances

"Everyone, please come to the center of the room," said Miss Drew. "And form a circle."

The class had finished their *barre* work, and their walks, leaps, and turns across the floor. They gathered around Miss Drew.

"What are we going to do now?" asked Ellie.

Miss Drew winked at Pat. "Dreadful day dances," she said. "Here's a question for you, class. Is ballet always happy?"

"It makes me happy," Mary answered.

"I saw a ballet called *Swan Lake*," said Paul. "It was sad. A magician turned a princess into a swan. A prince fell in love with her. But the magician tricked them. Then they died."

"I saw it, too," said his brother, Stanley. "The swans were pretty."

"Is ballet always pretty?" asked Miss Drew.

"My mom thinks it is," Pat answered.

"The men aren't pretty," said Paul.

"They're handsome," said Lynn. "I saw a ballet with a prince in it, too. He was handsome."

"The magician in *Swan Lake* was ugly," said Paul. "And mean."

"So, ballet can be happy and pretty," said Miss Drew. "But it can also be sad and ugly and mean."

"Wait till my mom hears that!" said Pat.

"Can ballet be anything it wants to be?" asked Ellie.

"Can it be scary?" asked Lynn.

"Let's see," said Miss Drew. "Who wants to dance 'scary' for us?"

"I do!" said Mary.

Everyone stepped back to give her

room. Mr. Ross played low, spooky notes on the piano. Mary curled her hands into claws. She twisted up her face and showed her teeth. She stomped around the circle, slashing at people with her claws.

Rosa and Sarah pretended to be afraid of her. The three of them danced together.

Pat wanted to dance, too. But she felt shy. Mary was the best dancer in the class. Everyone clapped for her when she finished.

"Is that a dreadful day dance?" asked Ellie, when they finished.

"Yes, it is," said Miss Drew.

"Why?" asked Ellie.

"You'll see," said Miss Drew. "Who wants to dance 'sad,' now?"

Pat knew all about "sad." It was exactly

how she felt. She wanted to raise her hand, but she just couldn't.

"How about you, Pat?" said Miss Drew.

Pat felt quivery as she stepped into the circle. She looked at the faces around her. Everyone was waiting for her to do something. But what? Mr. Ross played slow, quiet music. It sounded lonely.

"Think about a sad time, Pat," said Miss Drew. "And just move with the music."

Pat thought about the day her dad moved out. That was the saddest time of all. Her shoulders sagged. The corners of her mouth drooped. She remembered running to the window to wave good-bye. She ran out of the circle to the window. She pulled back a corner of the pink curtain.

She waved and waved and waved. Then she walked back to the circle, slowly. Her head hung low.

It felt a lot like the day her dad left. But it felt different, too. This time it wasn't really happening. She was just dancing.

"She's sad because somebody went away," Rosa said.

"She waved good-bye," said Nancy.

They sounded sad when they spoke.

"Very nice, Pat," said Miss Drew.

Pat smiled. She had done it right! They understood.

"Let's all dance 'sad,'" said Miss Drew.

Mr. Ross played more gloomy notes on the piano. The class moved slowly around the room.

"How about angry music, Mr. Ross?" said Miss Drew.

The low notes got loud and fast. Pat shook her fists. She rushed around the room, dancing angrier and angrier. But it didn't really feel like being angry. It felt like fun!

"Happy music, Mr. Ross," said Miss Drew.

The notes went up high. They seemed to be laughing. Miss Drew threw open her arms. She kicked up her heels. Mary turned cartwheels all around the room.

Pat skipped after her, clapping her hands. "I know why these are dreadful day dances!" she called to Miss Drew. "They make bad days feel better!"

"Remember that!" Miss Drew called back.

Chapter Four
The Second Promise

When the music ended, the whole class sank to the floor. Even Miss Drew. She folded her long legs, Indian style. "Ballet *can* be anything it wants to be," she said.

"Except boring," said Paul.

"That's right," said Miss Drew. "Do you know what's really boring? Dancers who don't know what they're doing. So let's practice our Circus Ballet for Visiting Day."

Visiting Day! There it was again. Just when Pat had almost forgotten.

Everyone jumped up and dashed into place for the Circus Parade. Pat dragged herself into line beside Ellie and Mary.

"We should have practiced," Mary whispered.

But it was too late. Mr. Ross began the parade music. Miss Drew pretended to be the ringmaster. She blew her whistle and snapped her whip. The elephants swayed around her. The monkey skipped. The horses pranced. The bear shuffled. The dog trotted. The lion stalked.

Then Nancy bumped into Sarah.

"Watch out!" said Sarah.

"Shhhh," said Miss Drew.

Lynn stepped on Rosa's toe.

"Ow!" yelled Rosa.

"Watch where you're going!" said Miss Drew.

Rosa grabbed her toe and hopped up and down. She crashed into Paul and Stanley.

"Quit it!" they yelled.

"Oh, no!" cried Miss Drew. "Stop! Stop! Stop!"

Pat, Ellie, and Mary were next in line. They couldn't stop prancing fast enough.

Mary knocked Stanley down. Then she fell
on top of him.

The Circus Parade music stopped.

Frowning hard, Miss Drew helped Mary

and Stanley to their feet. "What is going on?" she asked the class. "We're going to have an audience here next week. Your families and friends will be watching you.

Is this what you want them to see?"

No one answered. Pat hung her head. She peeked sideways at the rest of the class. Their heads were all hanging, too.

"Maybe you're nervous," said Miss Drew. "Don't be. If you pay attention, you'll do fine. Let's go on to the Animal Acts. Elephants, your dance comes first. Now, *think*!"

One by one, each kind of animal danced alone. Pat stood close to Mary and Ellie and watched. Paul and Stanley were funny elephants. But Rosa forgot her whole dog dance. Miss Drew had to help her with every step.

"Our turn," Pat whispered when Rosa was done.

She stepped forward to the music. So did Ellie and Mary. They bowed their heads and pawed the ground. Pat looked at the mirror. The three of them were moving together, just like circus horses. It was great!

Suddenly Ellie stopped. "What are you doing?" she asked Pat.

"Step, step, turn," Pat said.

"That's not what comes next," said Ellie. "This is where we gallop."

"No, we don't," said Pat.

"Yes, we do," said Ellie.

"Oh, let's not fight!" cried Mary.

"Then tell her we gallop," said Ellie.

"No! Tell *her* we step, step, turn," said Pat.

"Which is it?" asked Miss Drew.

"Oh, I don't know!" wailed Mary. "Now they have me all mixed up."

Miss Drew folded her arms. Her lips made a thin, angry line. "What is the one thing ballet cannot be?" she asked.

"Boring," said Paul.

"Yes," said Miss Drew. "And what is the most boring thing of all?"

"Dancers who don't know what they're doing," said Pat.

"Right!" said Miss Drew. "How many of you practiced your dances at home last week?"

Only Paul and Stanley raised their hands.

Miss Drew rolled her eyes. "We are out of time now," she said. "Go home and practice. Think about your dances when you can't practice. Dream about your dances when you sleep."

"We will!" said Pat. She had never seen Miss Drew so upset. It made her feel terrible. She couldn't let Miss Drew down.

"Promise?" asked Miss Drew.

"Yes!" said Pat.

And the whole class promised.

Chapter Five
Whispers

"Write each spelling word three times, please," Mr. Crane told his third-grade class on Monday morning. "Then write one sentence for each word."

Pat, Mary, and Ellie looked at each other and made faces.

Mr. Crane's bow tie was purple today. Pat liked his bow ties and his fuzzy white hair. Mr. Crane was nice, but he was strict, too. He had lots of rules.

"In cursive?" Ellie asked. She slapped one hand over her mouth and waved the other in the air. That was one of Mr. Crane's rules: Third-graders raise their hands before they speak. Ellie was always too full of questions to wait to be called on.

"In cursive," said Mr. Crane.

Pat took out a clean sheet of paper. She wrote her name at the top, in the right-hand corner. She wrote *Spelling* in the middle. Then she put a number one under that on the left side.

Mr. Crane walked up and down the aisles. "Ralph Major," he said. "Third-graders do their own work."

Pat and Ellie grinned at each other when Ralph got scolded. Ralph was the meanest boy in third grade. Ellie sat right behind

him, two rows away from Pat and Mary.

"Did you practice our dance at home?" Ellie asked Pat. She didn't say it out loud. She just moved her lips.

Pat shook her head. She and her mom had spent the rest of Saturday shopping and eating and going to the movies. On Sunday, they visited Pat's aunt and uncle.

"Ask Mary," Ellie said, with her lips.

Pat waited until Mr. Crane moved into the next aisle. Then she turned around in her seat.

"Ellie wants to know if you practiced," she whispered. "For Visiting Day."

"No," Mary whispered back. "We have to do it together."

"What's everybody whispering about?" asked Ralph Major. He asked it right out loud.

"I don't know, Ralph," said Mr. Crane. "But I think they should stop it."

Pat's face got red and hot. She went back to her spelling words. She did them all without stopping.

After that came silent reading. As Pat pulled a book out of her desk, Ellie waved at her.

"Did Mary practice?" Ellie asked. But not out loud, like Ralph.

"She said we have to do it together," Pat mouthed back.

"What?" Ellie asked.

"Together," Pat whispered, as softly as she could.

"Patricia Parker," said Mr. Crane. "Third-graders read silently during silent reading."

Pat blushed again. She put her book up close to her face. But she didn't even read the first word. Only five more days, she thought. They had to practice or their dance would be awful. They had promised Miss Drew.

Pat closed her eyes tight and thought about her father. He'll be able to come, she told herself. He will. He will. He will. Maybe she could make him come if she hoped for it hard enough.

Chapter Six
The Third Promise

"Time for recess," Mr. Crane announced. "Line up, third-graders. Walk, please."

Mr. Crane marched the class outside. Ralph Major caught up to Pat, Ellie, and Mary in the yard.

"So, what was all the whispering about?" he asked.

"None of your business," said Ellie. She and Ralph were always fighting.

"It's my business if I say it is," Ralph said. He gave Ellie a push.

Ellie pushed him back. "Leave us alone," she told him. "Go away."

Ralph moved two steps closer. "Tell me what you were whispering about," he said.

"We don't have to," Pat said.

"You do if I say so," said Ralph.

"You don't make the rules," Mary said.

Ralph hooked two fingers in his mouth and pulled his lips back, almost to his ears. Then he stuck out his tongue.

David Sims came up. "Anybody want to play kickball?" he asked.

Ralph pulled his tongue back in. "I do," he said.

"*We* can't," said Ellie.

"Why not?" asked David.

"I can't tell you," Ellie said.

"It's what they were whispering about in class," said Ralph.

"You can tell David," said Pat.

"No, I can't," said Ellie. "Ralph will hear. And it's none of Ralph's business."

"We're best friends, Ellie," David said. "We don't keep secrets."

"We do from Ralph," Ellie told him.

David's dark eyes got big and round. Pat

could tell he felt left out. She felt sorry for him. But she liked having a secret with Ellie and Mary.

Mary pulled Ellie and Pat into a huddle. "Our dance is a mess," she whispered. "If we tell them about it, they'll laugh."

"Every time Ralph hears 'Ballet One,'" said Pat, "he sticks his finger down his throat and pretends to throw up."

"Maybe we'd better keep our dance a secret," Mary said. "Until we get it right. Until Visiting Day."

"Okay," said Ellie. "Let's promise."

They all put their hands together and promised.

Ellie backed out of the huddle. "I can't tell you, David," she said.

"All right for you," said David. "Let's go, Ralph. *We'll* play kickball. Who needs *them?*"

Ellie looked glum as she watched David trot away with Ralph. But Pat was glad to see them go. "Come on, Ellie," she said. "We have to make plans. When can we practice together?"

"Not at school," said Mary. "Everyone will see."

"Then right after school?" asked Pat.

"I have to go to the dentist today," said Ellie.

"Tomorrow, then," said Pat. "At my house. My mom drives the car pool on Tuesdays. We can all squeeze in."

Chapter Seven
One Promise Broken

"You're very quiet tonight," Mrs. Parker said as she and Pat cleared the dinner dishes.

"I'm thinking about our dance," said Pat. "Miss Drew told us we should think about it when we can't practice it."

"Ballet sounds like hard work," said Mrs. Parker. "I didn't think it was. Dancers make it look so easy. They seem to float on air."

"It is easy," said Pat. "After you practice it a million times."

"Then you go practice," said Mrs. Parker. "I'll finish the dishes myself."

"Thanks, Mom!" Pat said.

She gave her mother a kiss on the cheek.

Then she ran into the living room. She practiced there until her mother came in. "No peeking until Saturday!" she said. "Okay?"

"Okay," said Mrs. Parker.

Just as she started back to the kitchen, the phone rang. Pat raced into the kitchen ahead of her. "Maybe it's Daddy!" she cried.

She skidded to a stop and answered the phone.

"Pattycake?" said Mr. Parker. "How's tricks?"

Pat closed her eyes and crossed all her fingers and toes. "Tricks are fine," she said. "Can you come?"

"I'm sorry, honey," said Mr. Parker. "The trip to Omaha is on."

Pat's mouth started to twitch. She bit her lip.

"Pat, I really wish I could be with you," her father went on. "Could you at least tell me about your dance?"

Pat didn't say anything. She couldn't.

Tears were burning her eyes and hurting her throat.

"Pattycake, are you there?" Mr. Parker asked.

"Yes," was all she could squeeze out.

"Maybe you don't feel like talking right now," her father said. "Well, I leave first thing in the morning. We'll talk Saturday night. Okay?"

"Okay," Pat whispered.

"I am sorry," said her father. "Love you."

Pat didn't answer. Everything felt squeezed tight, from her lips to her heart. Her father said good-bye and hung up.

Pat ran back to her room. She slammed the door shut. Then she threw herself across the bed.

There was a knock on the door. Mrs. Parker came in. "Let's talk, Pat," she said.

"No!" Pat cried. "He broke his promise."

"He didn't want to," Mrs. Parker said. "He had to."

"He didn't have to," Pat insisted. "If he

really cared about me, he would have kept it."

"Oh, Pat — " Mrs. Parker began.

But Pat pulled out her pillow and pressed it over her ears as hard as she could.

So what if he can't come? she told herself. Who needs him? I still have Ellie and Mary. We're best friends. We do everything together. Third grade and Ballet One and *secrets*. We'll practice our dance until it's great. And he won't get to see it. *Then* he'll be sorry!

Chapter Eight
Another Promise Broken

The next day, after math and spelling, Mr. Crane gave out orange and black paper. The class went to work on Halloween decorations for the room.

Pat cut out a giant pumpkin. She turned in her seat to show it to Mary. But she stopped halfway around. Ellie was dancing her fingers across the top of her desk.

Pat could tell what she was doing. Bow and turn. Gallop. Step, step, turn. Pat and Mary smiled at each other. It was a secret way to practice at school!

Before Mary and Pat could try it, too, Ralph looked up from the pumpkin he was drawing. "Hey, what's that drumming sound?" he yelled.

"Ralph Major," said Mr. Crane from the back of the room. "A third-grader who yells that loud had better have something worth yelling about."

"Ellie's drumming her fingers on her desk," Ralph said. "How can I draw pumpkins with all that noise?"

"You can't draw pumpkins when it's quiet," Ellie said.

"Ellen Bell," said Mr. Crane. "That was not helpful." He moved up the aisle toward his desk.

"When you're dumb, dumb, dumb, you have to drum, drum, drum," Ralph muttered.

Mr. Crane spun his finger in the air. He meant for Ralph to face front. "That's quite enough, Ralph," he said.

Ralph faced front.

"Ellen," said Mr. Crane, "would you like to explain to the class what you were doing?"

Ellie's face turned red. She looked at Pat. Then she looked at Mary. Then she looked back at Mr. Crane.

"Well?" he asked.

"I was practicing our dance for Ballet One," she said.

"Ellie!" cried Pat.

"Ballet One! Yuck!" yelled Ralph. He stuck his finger down his throat and pretended to throw up.

Suddenly everyone was talking at once. Mr. Crane frowned hard and raised one hand above his head. The class got quiet.

"Third-graders," Mr. Crane said. "You

have a choice. You may go right on chattering and miss recess. Or you may calm down and go outside to play."

The class stayed quiet.

"All right," said Mr. Crane. "Line up, please. No running."

Pat could hardly make herself walk slowly across the room. Mr. Crane seemed to take forever marching the class down the hall. The minute he let them go, she chased out the door after Ellie.

"You weren't supposed to tell!" she said.

Mary, David, and Ralph closed in around them.

"I had to," Ellie explained. "Mr. Crane made me."

"But you promised," said Pat. "You made us promise. It was your idea. I didn't even let my mom watch me practice."

"Don't fight," said Mary. "Ellie had to tell Mr. Crane. She couldn't lie."

"She didn't have to say *what* she was practicing," Pat insisted. "I think she *wanted* to tell."

"I did," Ellie admitted. "I don't like it when David's mad at me."

"Oh, who wants to hear about Ballet One anyway?" said Ralph.

"Stay out of this, Ralph," Ellie snapped.

"Oh, never mind Ralph," Pat said. "You're the one who broke a promise, Ellie. You can't do that!"

"I can, too," said Ellie. "I shouldn't have promised in the first place. It hurt David's feelings. And that's not fair. He's coming to see me on Visiting Day. He's even bringing his parents."

Pat fought back the tears that were aching in her chest. "A promise is a promise!" she yelled.

"I'm sorry," said Ellie.

"Sorry?" Pat cried. Tears stung her eyes. She was too angry to brush them away. "Sorry doesn't help. We're not best friends anymore, Ellie Bell."

"Oh, come on, Pat," Mary begged. "Don't be that way."

"I'm never talking to Ellie again!" Pat said. "Ever! So there!"

"What about our dance?" asked Mary. "What about practicing together?"

"You can both forget about coming to my house this afternoon," Pat said. "You can forget about our dance, too. I'm not dancing with anyone who breaks promises."

"You have to," said Mary. "We can't change our dance now. It's too late."

"I don't have to if I don't want to," said Pat.

"What'll you tell Miss Drew?" asked Mary. "You promised *her*."

"I'll just tell her I'm sorry," said Pat. "That's what everybody else does. Isn't it?"

Chapter Nine
Silence and a Souvenir

The whistle blew, and Mr. Crane waved everyone into line. No one said a word as they shuffled inside.

When Pat got to her desk, she sat down hard. Then she drew the meanest face she could on her pumpkin.

After school, Pat and Mary waited for Mrs. Parker with the rest of their car pool: a fifth-grade boy and two kids in afternoon kindergarten. Pat and Mary were so quiet, the other three just stared at them.

"Hi, everybody," said Mrs. Parker, as she pulled up to the curb. She opened both doors and helped the kindergartners into the backseat. "Where's Ellie?"

"She's not coming," Pat snapped, climbing in front.

Mary sat next to her. She looked out the side window all the way home. No one said another word.

The kindergartners were the last ones out. As soon as they were gone, Mrs. Parker asked, "What happened?"

"Nothing," said Pat. "Ellie and Mary and I are not best friends anymore. That's all."

Mrs. Parker pulled into the garage. She turned off the motor. "That's a lot," she said.

Pat did not want to talk about it. She was tired of feeling sad. She was tired of being angry. She was tired of everything. She got out of the car and went straight to her room.

She put away her sweater and book bag. Then she sat on the edge of her bed. She stayed there for a long time. There was nothing else to do.

The house sounded very quiet. Even the clangs and bangs of her mother getting dinner ready didn't seem noisy enough to fill it up.

There should be horses galloping around, Pat thought. There should be Ellie and Mary and giggling and dancing and planning. Even fighting would be better than this quiet.

They hadn't even decided which came first: the step, step, turn or the gallop.

It didn't matter now. There wasn't going to be any old horse dance anyway.

How could she ever tell Miss Drew that?

Pat picked up Fuzz, her best stuffed dog, and hugged him. She rubbed her cheek against his soft brown fur. That always made her feel a little better.

Then she remembered where Fuzz had come from. Her father had bought him for her at Silver Dollar City. He'd promised to take her there for her eighth birthday. And he did.

They went on every single ride. They watched all the shows. They visited every shop. And he bought Fuzz as a souvenir, to remember their day together. She hugged Fuzz tighter.

A little later, Mrs. Parker came to the door. "A penny for your thoughts," she said.

Pat put out her hand. Her mother pretended to drop in a penny.

"I'm thinking I should do some dreadful day dances," Pat said.

"What are those?" Mrs. Parker asked.

"Miss Drew says you can't always make other people do things your way," Pat explained. "She says sometimes you can only change your own feelings. Dreadful day dances cheer you up. They make bad days better."

"They do?" said Mrs. Parker. "I'd like to see that."

Pat slid off the bed, and Mrs. Parker sat down. Pat set Fuzz right beside her. Then she danced "angry" for the two of them.

It made her think of Ellie and the secret. She danced and danced until the angry feeling was all danced away. Ellie was right. A promise that hurt David was no good.

Then she danced "sad." That made her think of her father. It made her think he might be sad, too, about not being with her on Saturday. He said he was sorry. Maybe people said they were sorry when they broke a promise because they really were.

She stopped dancing. "I have to call Daddy," she said.

"He won't be home until Saturday night," her mother said.

"I'll call him then. Don't let me forget," Pat said.

"I won't," said Mrs. Parker.

Pat danced "scary." Mrs. Parker laughed and clapped her hands. Soon Pat was laughing, too. So she danced "happy." She picked up Fuzz and took her mother by the hand. They all skipped and twirled together. Fuzz leaped from the dresser to the chest of drawers and back.

When Pat and her mother were out of breath, they fell back on the bed, still laughing. Pat knew she could never break her promise to Miss Drew. Not after the dreadful day dances. Not even if she said "I'm sorry."

But she could tell Ellie and Mary she was sorry. She had to. They all had to keep their promise to Miss Drew.

"I think there are three kinds of promises," she told her mother. "The kind that shouldn't be made. The kind that can't be kept. And the kind that should be made and can be kept. Those are the ones to keep."

"I think you're right," said Mrs. Parker. She put her arms around Pat and Fuzz and held them tight.

"If I call Mary and Ellie, will you pick them up and bring them over after dinner?" Pat asked. "We need to practice."

"Sure," said Mrs. Parker. "Give them a call."

Chapter Ten
Visiting Day and Pat's Promise

"First we gallop," said Mary. "Then we step, step, turn. And *no more fighting!* Okay?"

Pat and Ellie looked at each other and giggled. "Okay," they said together.

They were all in Pat's living room after dinner. They were friends again. Mrs. Parker had helped them push back the coffee table and sofa so they could practice.

They practiced all that evening and the next and the next. "The dance is getting better and better," Mary announced on Thursday. "But I'm getting more nervous."

"Me, too," said Pat.

"My mom says no practicing tomorrow

night," said Ellie. "She says we should just get to bed early."

"I won't sleep," said Mary.

"Me, neither," said Pat.

But she did, with Fuzz tucked in beside her on the pillow. And then it was Saturday.

At Ballet One, two long rows of folding chairs were set up in front of the mirrors. They made the whole room look different. Pat felt even more nervous than before. Ellie and Mary grabbed her hands the minute she stepped in the door.

"Don't ever let go!" Mary begged.

Ellie laughed. But she was so excited, it came out a snort. "We'll have to let go to *dance*," she said.

A giggle tickled Pat's throat. "We'd better not laugh," she said. "What if we get the hiccups?"

"Hiccuping horses," said Ellie. And the three of them had to try even harder not to laugh.

Mrs. Parker sat right in the first row. So did David, Mr. and Mrs. Sims, and Ellie's parents. Behind them were Mary's parents and all four brothers, two big and two small.

"Line up, please," said Miss Drew.

Everyone hurried to the *barre*, just as if it were any other Saturday. Once the music began, Pat felt better. It *was* like any other Saturday. It was fun.

"You've seen our *barre* work," Miss Drew told the audience, at last. "And our work in the center of the room. Now we have something very special to show you. Ballet One presents its own Ballet Circus!"

The audience clapped. Pat stole a peek at her mother from her place in line. Her smile was the biggest in the room. It made Pat feel even better.

Mr. Ross began the Circus Parade music. Pat looked at Mary and Ellie. Ellie grabbed her stomach, where the butterflies were. Mary rolled her eyes. Pat grinned.

Miss Drew pretended to be the ringmaster. She blew her whistle and snapped her whip. The parade began.

It was like a dream. It was better than a

dream, because it was real. Pat forgot about the audience. She forgot to be scared. She floated from one part of the dance to the next. She remembered every step, even the step, step, turn and the gallop. So did the others.

Suddenly it was all over. The audience clapped and cheered.

"That was great!" David yelled.

Mrs. Parker jumped out of her seat. She wrapped Pat in a big hug. "Ballet One isn't at all what I thought it would be," she cried. "It's so much more! Elephants and horses and dreadful day dances and *everything*!"

"Ballet can be anything it wants to be," said Miss Drew.

"Except boring," Pat reminded her.

Miss Drew laughed and winked at Pat. "I don't think we were, do you?" she asked. "Ballet One I'm proud of you all."

"Let's all go to Swenson's for ice cream," said Mrs. Parker. "We can celebrate with double-dip cones."

And they did.

That night after dinner, Pat dialed her father's number. "Daddy?" she said. "It's Pat. How's tricks?"

"Pattycake!" cried Mr. Parker. "Tricks are fine. How's tricks with you?"

"Fine," said Pat. "Was your trip to Omaha okay?"

"It was," her father answered. "But I'm sure it wasn't half as much fun as Visiting Day. How did that go?"

"Great," said Pat. And she told him all about Miss Drew and Ellie and Mary and the Ballet Circus, step by step. "I wish you could have seen it, Daddy," she said.